ATHENA

GODDESS OF WISDOM, WAR, AND CRAFTS

BY TERI TEMPLE   ILLUSTRATED BY ROBERT SQUIER

Published by The Child's World®
1980 Lookout Drive • Mankato, MN 56003-1705
800-599-READ • www.childsworld.com

ISBN 9781503832558
LCCN 2018957541

Printed in the United States of America

About the Author
Teri Temple is a former elementary school teacher who
now travels the country as an event coordinator. She
developed a love for mythology as a fifth-grade student
following a unit in class on Greek and Roman history. Teri
likes to spend her free time hanging out with her family,
biking, hiking, and reading. She lives in Minnesota with
her husband and their golden retriever, Buddy.

About the Illustrator
Robert Squier has illustrated dozens of books for children.
He enjoys drawing almost anything, but he really loves
drawing dinosaurs and mythological beasts. Robert Squier
lives in New Hampshire with his wife, son, and a puggle
named Q.

CONTENTS

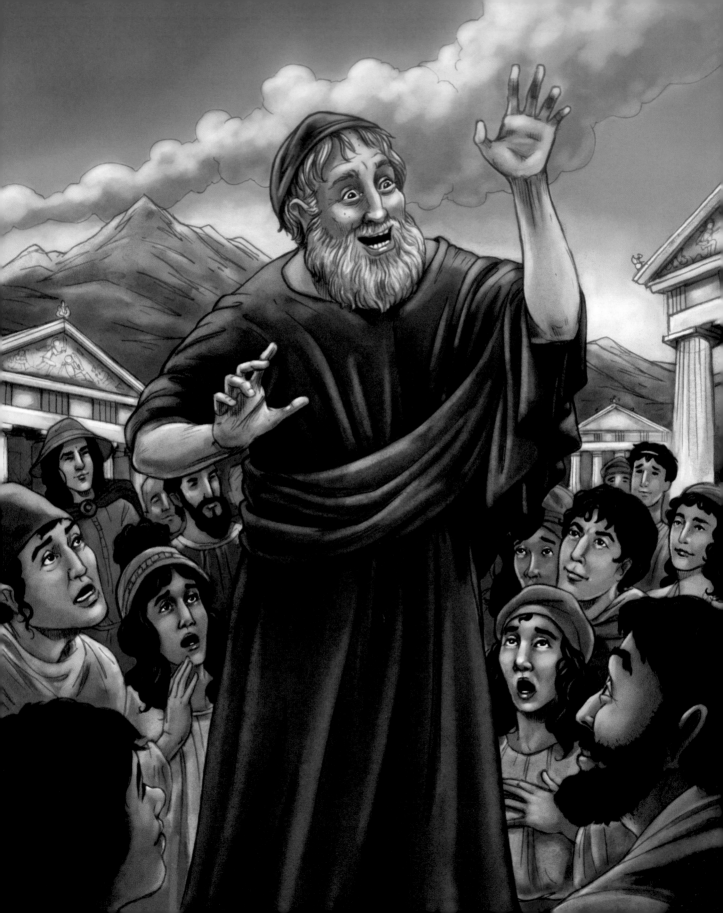

INTRODUCTION

Long ago in ancient Greece and Rome, most people believed that gods and goddesses ruled their world. Storytellers shared the adventures of these gods to help explain all the mysteries of life. The gods were immortal, meaning they lived forever. Their stories were full of love and tragedy, fearsome monsters, brave heroes, and struggles for power. The storytellers wove aspects of Greek customs and beliefs into the tales. Some stories told of the creation of the world and the origins of the gods. Others helped explain natural events such as earthquakes and storms. People believed the tales, which over time became myths.

The ancient Greeks and Romans worshiped the gods by building temples and statues in their honor. They felt the gods would protect and guide them. People passed down the myths through the generations by word of mouth. Later, famous poets such as Homer and Hesiod wrote them down. Today, these myths give us a unique look at what life was like in ancient Greece more than 2,000 years ago.

ANCIENT GREEK SOCIETIES

In ancient Greece, cities, towns, and their surrounding farmlands were called city-states. These city-states each had their own governments. They made their own laws. The individual city-states were very independent. They never joined to become one whole nation. They did, however, share a common language, religion, and culture.

MOUNT OLYMPUS
The mountaintop home
of the 12 Olympic gods

Aegean Sea

THEBES, GREECE
A city in Greece that
was built by Cadmus

ATHENS, GREECE
The capital of Greece;
patron city of Athena

*Mediterranean
Sea*

Sea of Crete

A N C I E N T
G R E E C E

C R E T E

CHARACTERS
AND PLACES

**ANDROMEDA
(an-DRAHM-uh-duh)**
Wife of the hero Perseus

ARACHNE (uh-RAK-nee)
A maiden who was turned
into a spider by Athena

CADMUS (KAD-muhs)
Greek hero who built
Thebes and was its first king

**CASSIOPEIA
(kas-ee-oh-PEE-uh)**
Mother of Andromeda;
constellation in the northern sky

CECROPS (SEE-krahps)
First king of Athens, Greece

GAEA (JEE-uh)
Mother Earth and one
of the first elements
born to Chaos; mother
of the Titans, Cyclopes,
and Hecatoncheires

GORGONS (GOR-guhnz)
Three monstrous
sisters with snakes for
hair; can turn men to
stone with their gaze

HEPHAESTUS (huh-FES-tuhs)
God of fire and metalwork;
son of Zeus and Hera;
married to Aphrodite

HOMER (HOH-mur)
Ancient Greek poet
from the eighth century;
wrote the epic poems the
Iliad and the Odyssey

MEDUSA (muh-DOO-suh)
A snake-haired creature whose
gaze can turn people to stone;
mother of Pegasus; killed by Perseus

METIS (MEE-tis)
First wife of Zeus;
mother of Athena

NIKE (NY-kee)
Goddess of victory;
friend of Athena

ODYSSEUS (oh-DIS-ee-uhs)
Greek hero featured
in the epic poems the
Iliad and the Odyssey

PALLAS (PAL-uhs)
Childhood friend
of Athena

PERSEUS (PUR-see-uhs)
Greek hero who killed
Medusa; married
to Andromeda

POSEIDON (puh-SY-duhn)
God of the sea
and earthquakes;
brother to Zeus

ZEUS (ZOOS) Supreme
ruler of the heavens
and weather and of the
gods who lived on Mount
Olympus; youngest son
of Cronus and Rhea;
married to Hera; father of
many gods and heroes

OLYMPIAN GODS
Demeter, Hermes,
Hephaestus, Aphrodite,
Ares, Hera, Zeus,
Poseidon, Athena, Apollo,
Artemis, and Dionysus

PARTHENON
Ancient temple of Athena
in Athens, Greece

TROJAN WAR
War between the ancient
Greeks and Trojans

THE GODDESS OF WAR

High atop a mountain, hidden behind the clouds was a palace of marble and gold. It was Mount Olympus, home of the Olympic gods. There were six gods in the beginning. They were the three brothers Poseidon, Hades, and Zeus. And there were the three sisters: Demeter, Hestia, and Hera. They ruled over the heavens and the earth. The youngest brother, Zeus, was the king of the gods. He had fought his father for control of the universe with help from his siblings. The battle lasted ten long years. When it finally ended, peace settled over the earth. The brothers drew lots to pick where they would rule. To draw lots is to pick an object that represents a choice. When you pick, the outcome is based on chance. Poseidon became god of the seas. Hades ruled the underworld. Zeus became god of the heavens and the earth.

Zeus wanted a queen to help him rule. He chose his cousin Metis as his first wife. She was known for her good counsel. She could offer Zeus advice that would help him be a fair and just king. Not long after their marriage, Metis discovered she was expecting their first child.

Everything seemed perfect until Gaea, or Mother Earth, warned Zeus of a prophecy. A prophecy is a prediction about the future. Mother Earth told Zeus that a child born to Metis would one day overthrow him. Zeus was worried! He had done the same thing to his own father.

Zeus knew he had to stop the birth. But he did not want to lose Metis's good advice, either. So he came up with a plan. He was sure it would take care of everything. Zeus challenged Metis to a shape-changing contest. He tricked her into becoming a tiny fly. Then he swallowed her up. Zeus foolishly thought all his problems were solved.

Many days later, Zeus began having horrible headaches. One day the headaches were so bad that he begged his son Hephaestus for help. Zeus asked Hephaestus to use his ax to split open his pounding head.

Always a good son, Hephaestus did as he was told. Athena popped out from the split in Zeus's skull. She was fully grown and dressed in full armor. Athena introduced herself to the world with a battle cry.

Athena was a grey-eyed beauty. She became Zeus's favorite child. He gave her a strong breastplate called the Aegis. A breastplate is a piece of armor that covers the chest. The Aegis would become one of Athena's greatest weapons. Zeus even let her hold his thunderbolts. Athena was known for her wisdom and justice. These skills would help her as the goddess of war.

Athena was a young woman. But she had trouble fitting in on Mount Olympus. So she set out to find her own place in the world. Athena found a friend in Pallas. She was a daughter of the sea god Triton. Together they often practiced their fighting skills. One day during training, Athena's blow accidentally killed Pallas. Deeply sorry for the accident, Athena wanted to remember her friend always. So she set a statue of Pallas near Zeus's throne on Mount Olympus. Athena also took on her friend's name. Her followers often called her Pallas Athena.

Nike was another of Athena's constant companions. Nike was the winged goddess of victory. Athena, in a golden helmet, was often seen on the battlefield with Nike. Together they fought for just causes. With her lance and shield, Athena led armies in times of war. But in times of peace, she was able to share her skills in the arts and crafts.

ANCIENT EDUCATION

Few girls attended school in ancient Greece, but many were taught to read at home. Most children learned some practical skills from their parents or slaves. The schools taught boys general studies, music, and physical education. Older boys also received training in handling weapons.

As the goddess of crafts, Athena was skilled at more than just fighting. She loved literature, poetry, music, and the arts. She also loved to invent things. She created the flute but never learned to play it very well. Athena's favorite invention was the loom for weaving. She loved to weave beautiful tapestries. A tapestry is a heavy cloth woven to show a picture.

A silly maiden named Arachne began claiming that her weaving was better than Athena's. Athena was furious.

SPIDERS

Many spiders can spin webs made of silk. This silk is made in the spiders' bodies. Spiderwebs can be simple or very complex in design. One purpose is to catch insects for food. Spiders are not insects, though. Insects have six legs, but spiders have eight. They are arachnids. The ancient Greeks believed that the first spider in the world was the maiden Arachne. The name *Arachne* means "spider" in Greek. From Arachne came the word arachnids, which is another word for spiders.

How could a simple girl compare herself to a goddess? So Athena challenged Arachne to a contest of skill. They each would be judged on one tapestry. Sitting at her loom, Athena created a perfect picture showing the splendor of the Olympian gods. Arachne's tapestry was also perfect. But Arachne's tapestry showed only how foolish the gods could be. Athena tore the tapestry to shreds in anger. She also turned Arachne into the first spider. Now Arachne would only weave spiderwebs.

Unlike other goddesses on Mount Olympus, Athena was too busy for marriage. Instead, she became the special friend to people in need. Heroes called upon her for protection. Cadmus would become one of those heroes. He was a foreign prince on a quest. Zeus had kidnapped his sister Europa. Cadmus sailed to Greece. An oracle told him that Europa was safe and well there. He was told by the oracle to end his search and stay in Greece to build a new city.

During the journey, Ares, the god of war, sent a dragon after Cadmus. The dragon attacked Cadmus and killed all of his men. Cadmus then killed the dragon. Athena told him to plant its teeth in a field. From the ground arose an army of warriors. So Athena told Cadmus to throw a stone amongst them to trick the warriors into attacking each other. The battle lasted until only five warriors were left. These five became the loyal servants of Cadmus. Together they built the city of Thebes. Cadmus became a great king and was favored by the gods. Zeus even gave Cadmus his daughter Harmonia in marriage. Thebes became one of the greatest cities in Greece.

Athena also showed favor to the handsome Perseus. He was a son of Zeus who was cast into the sea as an infant. Perseus had to fight to survive from the very start. He was sent by the king of Seriphus to collect the head of the Gorgon Medusa. This seemed an impossible task. Medusa could turn her enemies to stone with just a look. But Athena wanted Perseus to succeed.

Medusa had once been an attendant of Athena. Medusa had been very beautiful and caught the attention of Poseidon.

THE GORGONS

The Gorgons were three sisters. Their ugliness could turn men to stone. They were the daughters of the sea god Phorcys and the sea monster Ceto. The Gorgons' hair was a mass of hissing snakes. The ancient Greeks carved the Gorgons' image onto armor to terrify their enemies. They also felt the images protected them from evil spells.

He approached Medusa while she was visiting Athena's temple. She was enchanted by Poseidon's attention. When Athena discovered their affair, she was furious. As punishment, Athena transformed Medusa into a Gorgon. It was this creature that Perseus sought to kill.

Perseus was sure he would succeed with Athena at his side. Together they made a plan to slay Medusa. Zeus wanted Perseus to succeed as well. So he sent his son Hermes, the god of travels, to help.

Perseus traveled to the island of the Gorgons. He brought a bronze shield of Athena and a sword of Hermes. Athena had told him what to do when he arrived. He used the shield as a mirror to look at the sisters. Perseus saw the writhing snakes they had instead of hair. He also saw the stone statues of the men who had come before him. Perseus used the reflection to find Medusa and he beheaded her. He placed Medusa's head in a bag and planned to give it to Athena. But first he had to save the life of his future bride, Andromeda.

Her mother, Cassiopeia, dared to compare Andromeda's beauty to that of Poseidon's sea nymphs. In anger, Poseidon sent a horrible sea monster to destroy their home.

Andromeda was to be sacrificed to the monster. Her father chained Andromeda to the rocks in his kingdom of Ethiopia. On his way home, Perseus saw the beautiful maiden. He immediately fell in love. Perseus killed the monster using Hermes's sword. Together they returned to give Athena Medusa's head. Athena put the head onto her shield where it helped her in battle.

Athena found someone similar to herself in Odysseus. He was the Greek king of Ithaca. They shared many of the same qualities. Like Athena, Odysseus was smart, fair, and clever. He enjoyed Athena's protection during the Trojan War, but he really needed protection on his journey home.

The other gods wanted to punish Odysseus for defeating the Trojans. They had supported the Trojans during the war. So the gods created many problems for Odysseus as he sailed back to his wife and son. Odysseus was a prisoner of the sea nymph Calypso for seven years. After finally escaping, he sailed through storms and shipwrecks. Odysseus had angered the sea god Poseidon when he blinded his son Polyphemus. Athena did not want to anger the other gods. So she could only offer Odysseus guidance and advice in his dreams.

After ten long years, Odysseus finally returned to his home in Ithaca.

HOMER

Homer was a Greek poet who lived in the eighth century BC. He was thought to be blind. Homer is best known for his epic poems the *Iliad* and the *Odyssey*. They tell the tale of Odysseus, an ancient Greek sailor. The poems cover Odysseus's adventures as he sailed off to fight the Trojan War. Much of what we know about Greek mythology comes from Homer and his poems.

Athena warned him that many men wished to marry his wife. Since Odysseus had been gone so long, they were sure he was dead.

Athena helped disguise Odysseus. He then defeated more than 100 rivals. He regained his throne and his wife.

While the heroes celebrated Athena, her uncle Poseidon was often at odds with her. He was not a very clever god and was often frustrated by Athena. As the god of the sea, he wanted the waters for his creatures alone. Poseidon was furious when Athena taught men how to build ships. After that, humans sailed all over his oceans and seas. After Poseidon created the horse, Athena created the bridle and chariot. The chariot was a two-wheeled horse-drawn carriage. A bridle is made of straps and is used to control a horse. The bridle and chariot were used for hunting or racing. They also served the humans well in wars. Again Athena was shown to be more clever than Poseidon.

Then the day came when they each claimed the city-state of Athens. Athena and Poseidon both wished to become its patron. A patron is a protector of a place. Cecrops was the first king of Athens. He was half-human and half-snake. He came up with a contest to determine who it would be. Cecrops asked Athena and Poseidon to each offer a gift to the city of Athens. The winner would be the one whose gift was deemed most valuable. Poseidon was ready for the challenge.

Poseidon chose to go first. He wanted to prove his worth. He took his trident and struck the earth with it. A trident is a spear with three points. Poseidon was so powerful that water burst forth from the ground and formed a well. The people of the city were amazed. Their amazement did not last long, though. As the god of the sea, the water Poseidon had brought forth was salty. Cecrops did not think that would be too helpful to his city's people. Poor Poseidon was beside himself. Next up was Athena.

Athena used her spear to create a hole in the ground. She kneeled and planted an olive branch in the space. An olive tree grew from the branch. The ancient Greeks could harvest the olives for food. The people were very impressed with Athena's gift. Cecrops decided that Athena's gift was indeed more useful. He declared Athena the winner and the patron goddess of his city. The city was named Athens after Athena. In his anger, Poseidon caused the whole area to flood. Eventually though, Athena and Poseidon would work together for the sake of the people.

Nearly everyone loved and worshiped Athena. As the goddess of war she was often sought out for her sound judgment and good counsel. She was also a fierce warrior. She was sure to gain victory in battle with Nike at her side. Temples and shrines were built all over Greece in her honor. Festivals were held during the summer. The ancient Greeks gathered to pay tribute to Athena with competitions in athletics and music.

The most famous temple to Athena was the Parthenon. The Parthenon was an ancient temple in Athens, Greece. It was built between 447 BC and 432 BC. It sat on a hill known as the Acropolis above the city. The ancient Greeks dedicated the temple to Athena because she was the patron goddess of their city. The temple once held a great statue of the goddess covered in gold and ivory. Although her temple now stands in ruins, Athena remains an important part of the history of ancient Greece. Her stories will continue to be told for years to come.

MINERVA

Minerva was one of ancient Rome's most important goddesses. Rome conquered Greece in the third to second century BC. The Romans adopted many aspects of Greek culture. They especially liked the Greeks' stories about the gods. Athena became their goddess Minerva.

PRINCIPAL GODS OF GREEK MYTHOLOGY
A FAMILY TREE

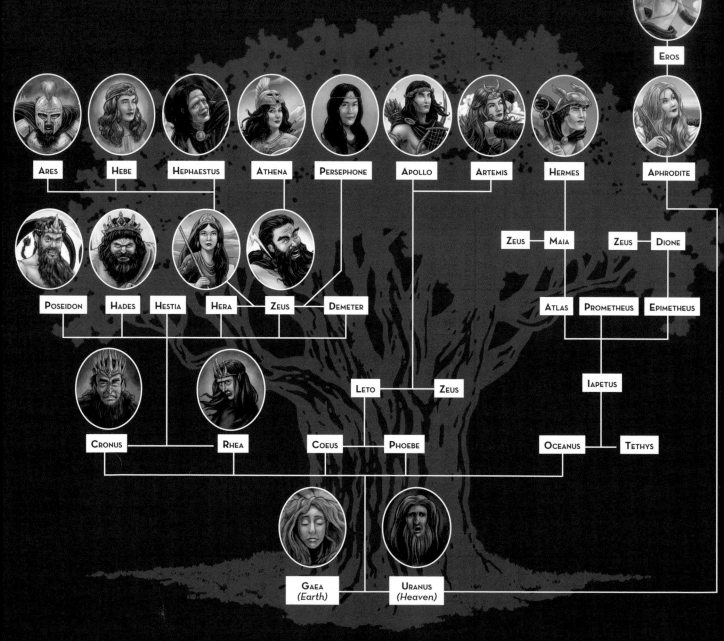

EROS

ARES HEBE HEPHAESTUS ATHENA PERSEPHONE APOLLO ARTEMIS HERMES APHRODITE

ZEUS — MAIA   ZEUS — DIONE

POSEIDON HADES HESTIA HERA ZEUS DEMETER   ATLAS PROMETHEUS EPIMETHEUS

IAPETUS

CRONUS RHEA   LETO ZEUS   COEUS PHOEBE   OCEANUS — TETHYS

CRONUS   RHEA   COEUS PHOEBE   OCEANUS TETHYS

GAEA
(Earth)   URANUS
(Heaven)

THE ROMAN GODS

As the Roman Empire expanded by conquering new lands, the Romans often took on aspects of the customs and beliefs of the people they conquered. From the ancient Greeks they took their arts and sciences. They also adopted many of their gods and the myths that went with them into their religious beliefs. While the names were changed, the stories and legends found a new home.

ZEUS: Jupiter
King of the Gods, God of Sky and Storms
Symbols: Eagle and Thunderbolt

HERA: Juno
Queen of the Gods, Goddess of Marriage
Symbols: Peacock, Cow, and Crow

POSEIDON: Neptune
God of the Sea and Earthquakes
Symbols: Trident, Horse, and Dolphin

HADES: Pluto
God of the Underworld
Symbols: Helmet, Metals, and Jewels

ATHENA: Minerva
Goddess of Wisdom, War, and Crafts
Symbols: Owl, Shield, and Olive Branch

ARES: Mars
God of War
Symbols: Vulture and Dog

ARTEMIS: Diana
Goddess of Hunting and Protector of Animals
Symbols: Stag and Moon

APOLLO: Apollo
God of the Sun, Healing, Music, and Poetry
Symbols: Laurel, Lyre, Bow, and Raven

HEPHAESTUS: Vulcan
God of Fire, Metalwork, and Building
Symbols: Fire, Hammer, and Donkey

APHRODITE: Venus
Goddess of Love and Beauty
Symbols: Dove, Sparrow, Swan, and Myrtle

EROS: Cupid
God of Love
Symbols: Quiver and Arrows

HERMES: Mercury
God of Travels and Trade
Symbols: Staff, Winged Sandals, and Helmet

FURTHER INFORMATION

BOOKS

Greenberg, Imogen. *Athena: The Story of a Goddess*. London: Bloomsbury Children's Books, 2018.

Napoli, Donna Jo. *Treasury of Greek Mythology: Classic Stories of Gods, Goddesses, Heroes & Monsters*. Washington, DC: National Geographic Society, 2011.

O'Connor, George. *Athena: Grey-Eyed Goddess*. New York, NY: First Second, 2010.

WEBSITES

Visit our website for links about Athena:
childsworld.com/links

Note to Parents, Teachers, and Librarians: We routinely verify our Web links to make sure they are safe and active sites. So encourage your readers to check them out!

INDEX